W9-CLK-661

THE PARTY

Barbara Reid

Scholastic Press · New York

To absent friends.

Photography by Ian Crysler
Copyright © 1997 by Barbara Reid

Library of Congress Cataloging-in-Publication Data
Reid, Barbara.
The party / Barbara Reid. p. cm.
Summary: Two sisters don't want to go to the annual family summer party,
but after they get there, they have so much fun, they do not want to leave.
ISBN 0-590-97801-2
[1. Family life—Fiction. 2. Parties—Fiction. 3. Stories in rhyme.] I. Title
PZ8.3.R2665Pat   1999   [E]—dc21 98-29778   CIP   AC

10 9 8 7 6 5 4 3 2   9/9 0/0 01 02 03
Printed in Mexico   49
First American edition, April 1999

The illustrations for this book were made with
Plasticine that was shaped and pressed onto illustration board.
Acrylic paint and other materials were used for special effects.

Me and my sister all dressed up to go.

Today is the day of the party.

Our friends are out playing.
We had to say no.
We're on our way to the party.

We are stuffed in the car
with a cooler, some chairs,
a bowl full of dip,
and a tin full of squares.

Squirmy and shy
by the end of the ride,
we take a deep breath
and step inside. . . .

"Here you are! Come on in!
Look how you've grown!"
There's no way to miss
being kissed by Aunt Joan.

The very worst part of the party.

People pile in.
More kissing. More fuss.
We look at the other kids.
They look at us.

How do we start at the party?

"I cut my own hair," Claire begins.
"Mommy cried."
Sally has stitches:
"I flew off the slide!"
Ben lost a tooth
when his launcher derailed.
Kate split her lip
'cause her parachute failed.
We all claim our fame at the party.

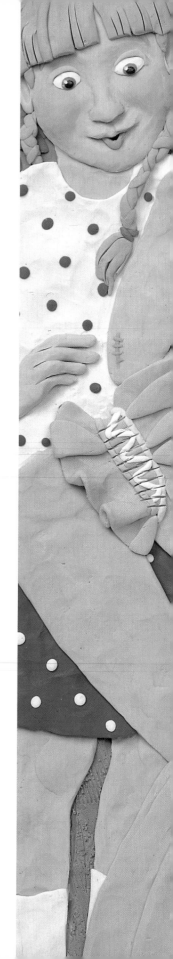

"Want to play sharks?" Danny asks.
Yes, we do!
"I'll be It. If I catch you,
then you're a shark, too!"

The lawn chairs are lifeboats,
the grass is all water.
Kate leaps to the birdbath —
too late! Danny's got her.
We're all in the game at the party.

I zip through the crowd
with the sharks on my tail.
Spring to the deck:
"Up anchor! Set sail!"
Then a tidal wave washes us all out to sea,
and the only survivors are Simon and me,
hiding deep in the hedge at the party.

Safe in our hideout
we're planning a raid.
Slip past the dragon —
we're not afraid.

Then slowly, so slowly,
on tiptoe we creep. . . .
Reach for the treasure chest:
"Now! He's asleep!"
Steal away to the edge of the party.

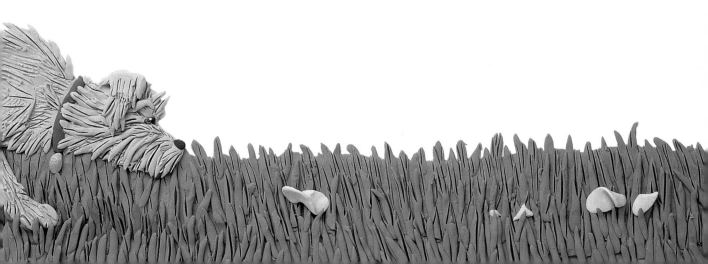

They call us: "Come eat!"
In a minute — we're busy!

We're spinning in circles
until we get dizzy.
We laugh till it hurts at the party.

But . . .
there are sausage rolls,
casseroles,
pineapple rings.
Deviled eggs,
chicken legs,
little cheese things.
Salads with jelly,
salads with beans.
Enough? Let the dog
lick your party plate clean.
Leave room for dessert at the party.

Happy birthday to you!
My favorite song.
Happy birthday to you!
Put your party hat on!

Happy birthday, dear Gran,
"Make a wish!" we all shout.
Happy birthday to you!
And we blow them all out.
We all give a cheer at the party.

Gran cuts the cake.
"Step right up, get your share!"
We make an escape
under Uncle John's chair.

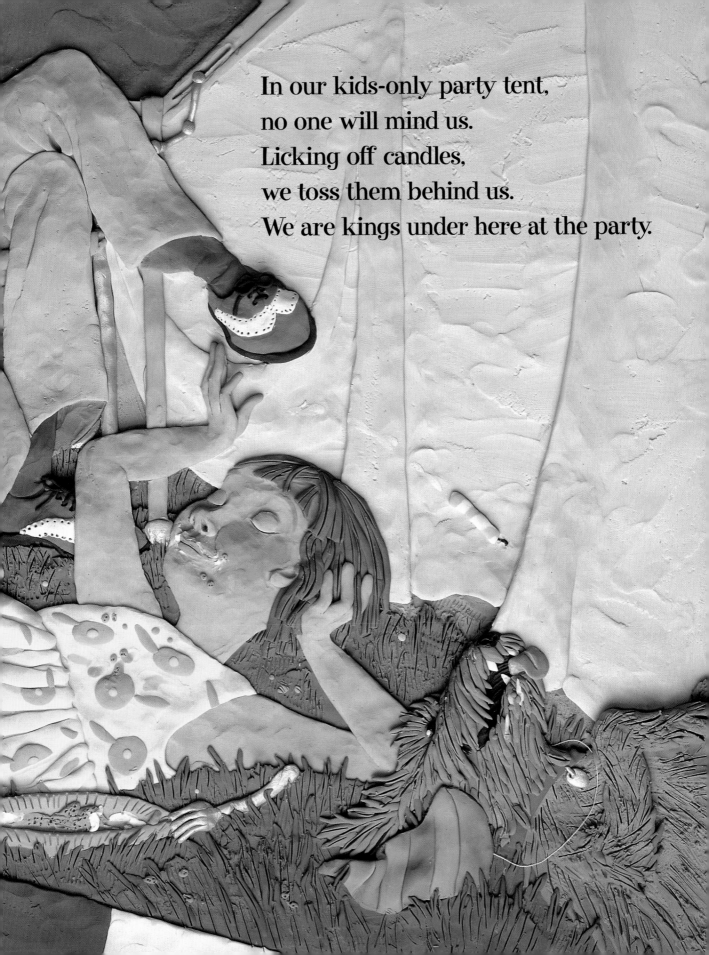

In our kids-only party tent,
no one will mind us.
Licking off candles,
we toss them behind us.
We are kings under here at the party.

The night air invites us
to enter the race —
a galloping wide-open heart-thumping chase!
Lopsided cartwheels collide in the air.
We all fall down giddy
with grass in our hair.

Then Ben says, "Look out!"
and I signal the others.
It's time to play hide-and-go-seek
from our mothers!

"We can't go right now!"
"One more game!"
"Can't we stay?"
But the grown-ups are
putting the party away. . . .

The cake is all gone.
No more tag or red rover.
My sister's in tears at the party.
Just time for good-byes
and the fun is all over.
We'll see you next year at the party.

It's way past our bedtime.
The streetlights are on.
We load up the car
and we try not to yawn.
Oh, what a great time,
what a wonderful time,
such a very late time
at the party.